good deed rain

The Orphanage of Abandoned Teenagers ©2017
Allen Frost, Good Deed Rain
Bellingham, Washington
ISBN 978-1-64008-160-4

Writing: Allen Frost
Cover photos & drawings: Allen Frost
Cover design: Fred Sodt
Cone model: our noble beast, Zoe
Apple: TFK!
Production assistance: Fred Sodt

"It's so hard to explain.
Sometimes it seems as if
I belong to a different world."

—*The Mummy's Curse*
Universal Studios, 1944

The
ORPHANAGE
of ABANDONED
TEENAGERS

Allen Frost

1.
REBECCA

I woke up. There's a car outside. I heard the motor and a door slam. Then in a rush for what remained of the night, the car roared away. There was silence on the street below, but I knew someone was waiting out there. The clock read 2:02.

I guess that means it's Monday morning. I forced myself to get up. My wife was asleep. I passed the window on my way around the bed and saw the streetlight, lonely as a candle. Whoever was left out there was probably on the porch.

I quickly put on my robe and headed downstairs. I knew what to expect on the other side of the door. This scene has repeated many times before.

Our dog Charles stood in the hall, thumping her tail in a wag against the wall. With the big plastic cone on her head, she has trouble negotiating the dimensions of our house.

I reached in the cone and scratched her.

"Good dog."

Charles is an old dog, but she wanted to let me know she was still on guard. She whimpered and turned her flower shaped head towards the door.

"Is someone there?" I whispered. "Should we find out?"

I could already see there was. The window in the door showed someone sitting on the top step. Long hair flowed over the back of a thick parka, with a suitcase on either side, facing the street like someone waiting for a taxi ride.

I turned the handle and the sound made the girl out there turn.

"Hello," I said.

Even though it was June, it was a cool night, quiet and shadowy.

I felt the cone scrape past my leg as Charles stepped onto the porch.

The girl smiled and held out her hand. The sight of Charles managed to be both sympathetic and comical and just what the girl needed at this moment.

"That's Charles," I said.

"Awww," the girl cooed and rubbed Charles' curly fur. "What happened to him?"

"She had to get stitches. She'll be okay though."

"Her name is Charles?"

"Long story," I said.

She laughed.

Charles thumped her yellow tail against the porch railing.

"You're a good dog, Charles," the girl said. Then she told both of us, "I'm Rebecca."

"Nice to meet you," I said. "I'm Leopold."

Charles could stand there until dawn getting pet, but my bare feet were cold and I brushed at a mosquito.

"How many other people besides me are here?" Rebecca said.

"Oh, there's me and Angie my wife, and just one boy, Steven. He's up in the tower room. He picked that room. You can pick one too. There are four other rooms to choose from."

"I don't know how long I'll be here."

"That's alright. You can stay as long as you want."

"They just make me so mad." She stared at the empty street. "They don't understand. They said they would take me here and I said fine. Do it."

Charles felt the petting stop and knocked her cone into a suitcase as she quickly swiveled.

"Well," I said, "As you can tell from Charles, we're glad you're here."

Rebecca stood up. She gave Charles another scratch then took hold of her two suitcases.

"You ready to find a room?" I asked.

She nodded.

I turned and opened the door. A long hallway led to the kitchen. The lamp on the table in there stays on at night and it glowed like a distant lighthouse.

Charles started inside ahead of us.

Almost like a museum, paintings and photos line the hall. A stairway leads upstairs to the left and down the hall to the right a doorway goes to the parlor. A door further down opens to the steep cellar stairs.

I helped Rebecca with her bags. "We can go upstairs and you can choose your room."

Charles turned around awkwardly to watch us climb, something the cone prevents her from doing easily. When she was a pup she would be the first one up the steps, but like me, she is getting old.

"Goodnight, Charles," I whispered. I stopped at the second floor landing. I hoped Rebecca wouldn't want to keep going up; her bags weren't exactly light. "There's a room down there at the end of the hall. It overlooks the garden in back."

"That sounds nice," she said to my relief.

We passed the bathroom and got to her room. I set down a suitcase and opened the door.

Every day we made the bed and cleaned the room in case someone would arrive. There was a pitcher on the dresser filled with wild flowers and Rebecca eyed the bed. "This is perfect," she said.

"Good. Sleep well. If you want anything, we're in the other room down the hall. When you wake up, come downstairs. Angie will be looking forward to meeting you."

"Thanks."

"And I know Charles will be waiting to see you in the morning too," I added. "Have good dreams."

She smiled.

I waved and left her room. It was hard to imagine the scene an hour ago, what must have brought such a sweet quiet girl here in the middle of the night. But I have seen her type before. Sometimes I would see them leave their parent's car yelling. Then once they got in here, quiet as a portrait. You would barely know they could speak. I don't know if they save up all their sound when they're out in the world and then by the time they get home it can't stay bottled up and they just explode.

That's why we're here. When it gets to that point, our house is here as a calm place of refuge. Sometimes all it takes is a night. She might be on the phone first thing in the morning, ready to go home.

I pushed our bedroom door open. I glanced at the clock. There were still a few more hours before I had to start for work. I got back in bed. A couple minutes passed while I listened to the night under the roof.

I was falling asleep as I heard an owl. Close by, it must have been in the fir just beyond the window. I wanted to keep listening, but I was so tired. I heard the owl one more time and then I don't know where the time went.

Next thing I knew it was daylight and the songbirds were calling up and down the street.

2.
THE CASTLE OF HAUNTED TEENAGERS

The Orphanage of Abandoned Teenagers. That's what I call it. I don't mean to make light of the situation—there seems to be no end to the need for a place for them. A little separation, a room of their own, but with others like them around. Sullen and moody, they are dropped off at the doorstep, usually at night. It's a particular type of teenager who shows up here. These aren't the rebellious or outward ones you see striking poses downtown, and not runaways with a will to survive. These teens are like museum butterflies stuck with the pins of their own making, whose suffering makes their life and their family's lives unbearably hard. They need help. These teens are still too scared to leave home but finding it harder and harder to stay there. They are stuck in a precarious time, moving out of childhood into adulthood and for some it's just the most difficult thing in the world. Their parents don't know what to do either—they're standing on the other side.

What the parents and the child really need is this orphanage. Their children stay until they want to go back home. It's usually only a night or two. And they have taken their first flight from the nest.

There are all kinds of young people coming here. Enough drama for a TV show. I should pitch that idea to my friend Count Misfit—he could be the host. It could be called *The Castle of Haunted Teenagers*. Each week would be a different story. Hmm...The Count already has a show, but if he ever needs a new program, we've got plenty of material.

Like the girl who broke her legs falling off a horse. When she was here last summer, I propped her in a lawn chair. She made friends with the deer in the corner of the garden. Anytime I look over there, I think of her. I bet the deer miss her too.

Some of our visitors have hidden talents they're so shy about. You might never know it's there, like going deep to find a buried ruby. The orphanage gives them a chance to shine.

In our basement, a boy made a model of a town on the moon. He said he saw the town

in a cartoon world

in his telescope and recreated the whole thing for me to see—the streets, the little houses and backyards and a pond he made from a broken piece of mirror.

One girl we had here carried a doll everywhere she went, talking to it, at the table, on the couch, caring for it. There's a magic to believing cloth is real. I hope that soon she will find that magic in something really real. She had so much feeling in her just waiting. When the Japanese maple was slow to show its spring red leaves, she made a rainbow of origami leaves for it.

We share simple little jobs around the house. One time we were doing the dishes after dinner and this boy arrayed everything clean like the letters in a poem. I was afraid to touch the stack. Even after they were dry. He had given them such a purpose and beauty.

There was a girl who wanted to live in a cartoon world with all her colorful, adorable friends. Her drawings made them alive. That place was all she thought about. I wonder if she ever made it there.

They are even getting in my dreams.

A girl who thought she was a bird arrived for the night. In the morning the bedroom window was open. A silent neighborhood outside. I looked at all the roofs and treetops. No sign of her. I hoped it was true, that she flew. It was a long drop to the garden.

Sometimes we go underground. Behind the back wall of the grocery store there's a tall cliff. It's covered in blackberry, but that's where you can find the old wooden door to the coal mines.

Another time it was a peaceful dream out on Lake Samish. I was paddling a canoe, staring at the swirl of current each time the blade left the water, and I was followed by a mermaid and her daughter.

I also dreamed I met myself. This would be the perfect story for *The Castle of Haunted Teenagers*. I don't know how I showed up at the door. How could I possibly be in two places at once? I guess because we weren't really the same. Before me stood my teenage version and I am nearly an old man. But I remembered him and I remembered what it was like. How could I forget? We didn't say much, he was quiet and polite. I showed him to a room. By daylight, the other me was history.

3.
COFFEE

I was on my way to work in a blizzard. After a long warm winter, I used the windshield wipers to clear the drifting cottonwood snow. It looked like December the way the branches were coated white on the parked cars and window sills. The sidewalks needed sweeping.

Bayview Cemetery was a mile or so from our house, maybe two. By the time I reached Bay Street, it was another temperate zone and the snow was gone, lost in the shuffle of cars.

When I left the house it was still quiet, no sign of Rebecca or Steven, but teenagers on their own don't often get up before seven. My wife would probably be stirring. She would make herself tea and be waiting for them. I must have told her something about our new guest Rebecca. I think I did. I yawned and turned the car at the entrance to the cemetery.

I'm sure it sounds interesting to be working at a cemetery. But don't imagine me out on the grounds with a shovel and a pet raven—I work in an office. It's inside a small brick building surrounded by shading trees. Really, it's just like any other job. Except most of the people I see arriving every day, I will never see again.

Oh, one time though, a ghost followed me home. It was hiding in the lining of my jacket and I didn't see it until I wondered why my jacket was so cold. I guess I should have known.

I parked in my usual spot next to Count Misfit's old finned automobile monstrosity. After his TV show, he sometimes caught a nap in there. Like one of the mad scientists in the movies he showed, he would creep out of his metal crypt after dawn and make strong black cemetery coffee. The aroma of it waited in the ivy around the office door.

It wasn't easy getting up early for work, especially when your house was filled with teenage tribulations. Coffee helped. The thought of it reminded me of a girl who stayed with us a little while. These days she's a well-known musician. I've seen her posters on telephone poles when she's in town. Back before then, when she couldn't sleep we used to walk to the

Miss B diner and share coffee. We talked about what it was like being an artist. And now she's on the radio with a traveling show.

Birds made the cemetery grounds seem like a cheery place. Maybe they had no idea what we did on this plot of earth, or maybe they gathered here because of it. I like to think they are radios tuned to play the songs we need to hear.

It wasn't long ago we had a boy stay with us who was obsessed with birds. He brought four suitcases with him, filled with instruments of his own making. In that same room of Rebecca's, he assembled all the pieces for a bird orchestra. At first light, when the backyard air was filling with songbirds, he played his composition. He told us about all the hours he spent listening to birds, transcribing their unique language into musical notes he could play back to them. He thought it would create a conversation. What was his name? I'm sorry I can't remember at the moment. He was a nice kid and very talented, but when that windowsill started to shake, the morning air seemed to tear with the sound he made.

I really don't understand how he believed his traffic jam of sound had any resemblance to birds. It was so raucous I felt I would have to ask him to stop. I was afraid the police would arrive. We listened numbly with buzzing ears, but the outdoors was a shrill silence. He scared every single bird away from the neighborhood. And it took weeks for them to come back.

The birds this morning were happy though. As usual they transformed all the feeling of a cemetery into layers of pleasant song.

I paused at the office door with my hand on the frozen handle. Like a welcoming butler, The Count's coffee greeted and ushered me inside.

The desk where I work waited for me, standing there in the gloom like a cow with a typewriter saddle. The door shut itself behind me with a click.

A wooden clock on the wall ticked time away.

Everything comes to an end, washing up against my desk. I offer what comfort I can to the families and grievers who arrive. That's my job.

In a way, it's not that different from what I do at the orphanage. When they show up, those teenagers are distraught. They don't know what's coming next, they are afraid—while life is waiting for them to step forward and join the parade.

I drifted around my desk. I wasn't ready for it yet. A door with pebbled glass glowed like a rocky shore. That was the way to coffee. Like someone in a trance, I was lifted off the ground and carried by that coffee's magnetic pull through the doorway.

The hall was lit by a 60 watt bulb suspended on a wire from the ceiling. There were two doors—one to the breakroom, and one that led to The Count's lab. Believe it or not, I've never gone in there. Why would I? I've seen the movies he hosts on KGUS. I can imagine it's some sort of Frankenstein lair, with crazed electrical equipment and a body on a slab awaiting lightning. All I know for sure is that behind that other door lies a shadow.

I'm reminded of that old riddle about the two doors. Behind one of them is a beautiful woman, behind the other is a tiger. How were you supposed to choose the right door? No…that can't be right. That would be too easy. Couldn't you just knock on the door and ask? If a woman answers, you know which door it is. Unless the tiger can talk too—is that what made it a riddle? Obviously I don't quite remember that story. I stopped at the breakroom door, the one that smelled like coffee, and pushed it open.

No tiger, no woman—it was only The Count, sitting at the table, reading a book.

Is it hard to believe that Count Misfit has a day job at the cemetery? It shouldn't be a surprise. The movies he shows on TV feature ghosts, monsters, rocket ships, time travel and other worlds. He goes from there to here seamlessly, but sometimes there's some green make-up left on his skin.

He held up his arm in a wave though his eyes were glued to the paperback. He had to finish the page. That was fine with me—I was after the coffee.

I caught a yawn in my hand on the way to the counter. The breakroom isn't much—a table, a couple chairs and a sink with a cupboard. A glass coffee urn sat awaiting me. It hissed like a black cat as I lifted it over to pour a cup.

4.
BLUE TYPEWRITERS

I spent the rest of the day sitting at the desk. I stay busy a fair amount of the time. There are always plenty of forms and the filing cabinets wait to be filled. I answer the phone and help people coming here. And all the usual office things too: scheduling and arrangements, sorting mail, keeping track of staff out on the grounds, reports and records and timesheets and etc. I had to take a typing test as part of the application. The requirement was 40 words per minute. Tap, tap, tappity, tap. That wasn't a problem for me. I've been playing that music for years. It's just as much a part of me as a functioning heart. In fact, that's where I first fell in love, with a girl in high school typing class. What a perfect setting. A whole room filled with blue typewriters. I think I talked with her twice. About the weather or some nervous thing.

When it's slow or whenever I get the chance, I type this book. I don't know if what I have to say will make it off the ground. We'll see if it gets published. You never know what will make it and what won't. You just have to try. That's what I tell the teenagers at the orphanage, even if all they do is sigh in reply.

We do have a library too. It's full of guidebooks. Hopefully this book will join them. I know that stores sell an awful lot of them. People are always looking for help raising kids. I have plenty of stories to tell and maybe some advice to give. It seems like forever, but time goes by much faster as we age. Keep trying to help, keep trying to stay calm, keep trying all over again.

My hands were resting on the typewriter keys, waiting for the next sentence.

Being an author, it was easy to daydream. I always have high hopes for the books I write. I've written a lot of other kinds of books, but with this one I'm really branching out. This one is different, this book is supposed to actually help people. This is about real life.

The sound of the telephone made me jump. "Boggs Funeral Service," I quickly answered. "May I be of assistance?"

"Hi. It's me."

"Hello. How are things at the orphanage?"

My wife sighed, "You're still calling our house that?"

I smiled, "Just wait until I finish my book about it. It will put us on the map." I switched the phone to my other ear. "Have I missed any exciting developments?"

"Well, Steven's parents picked him up this morning. I've been spending time with Rebecca."

Truthfully, my wife does most of the work around the orphanage. I go to work all day at the cemetery, while she feeds the teenagers, cares for them and washes load after load of laundry. When I get home, the long day at the office has tired me out, my strength has been sapped like the syrup from a maple tree.

"How's she doing?" I asked.

"Good. She's been a big help. Right now she's in the backyard using the typewriter."

That would be the old typewriter I set up on the patio. It used to be attached to a whirligig so that when the wind blew, it tapped out letters. Mostly it appears to only spell out some weird indecipherable code, but there was a time when that wasn't so. Words were blown into it. Someone we lost spoke to us. I may write about that later, I'm not sure. It would probably be interesting, it's just hard to talk about.

I was glad Rebecca was making use of it. "What's she typing?"

"She's making a job resume. Maybe you could take her out when you get home so she can turn it in?"

"Oh…Okay."

"She said she wants to work at the laundromat."

Of course I knew where that was, it wasn't far from home. We could walk there. I like going to the laundromat. I thought of it as an aquarium. "Tell Rebecca I can't wait."

"I'll tell her. See you soon."

"Okay. Adios." I hung up the phone and looked at the one little window in the room. Another sunny June end of the day at the cemetery.

5.
THE LAUNDROMAT HERO

Charles and I waited for Rebecca in the warm glow of the front yard garden. I watched a yellow butterfly. There was a breeze and I was amazed that something so papery could fight its way along from flower to flower. It could have been a poem that fluttered out of some book, moving like parade confetti over the sidewalk and gone.

The screen door opened and Rebecca called out to me, "I'm ready!" She wasn't kidding. She had her resume shut inside a slim briefcase and she wore a green summer dress.

I waited for her at the gate while she hopped and hurried down the path. If she had wings, she would be up in the leaves with the butterflies.

Angie appeared at the door and waved. "Good luck! Remember what we talked about."

Rebecca spun and called back, "I will!"

"See you," I waved to my wife. It felt like Rebecca and I were off on some fairytale journey. She carried typed directions to where she had been and what she did, and what she hoped to do. It was a road I had been down many times since I was her age. I was sort of lost in that thought when she read my mind.

"What was your first job?"

I laughed. "I was just trying to remember." I had to throw myself down a long well. The flowers crowding up through the sidewalk cracks reminded me. They cupped leafy hands and sang like an old cartoon. "Oh yeah...After school, I used to go to work at a nursery."

"With babies?"

"No, a plant nursery. Baby plants. They grew in big greenhouses. That was actually a pretty good job. I liked digging my hands in the earth."

"And now you work at a cemetery," she said, wrinkling her nose.

I couldn't help a laugh. "That's true. That is ironic how that worked out." I thought for a moment, looking at the fresh spring leaves of a passing tree. "So if you start at a laundromat, where will you end up?"

"Hmm," she wondered, "Somewhere else doing something with water?"

A dog bounced along the picket fence beside us.

Charles pulled her leash. Her muffled bark trumpeted out from the cone. It was like pulling on a fishing line, hauling her past that barking fence. The little bouncing dog made sure we wouldn't forget and kept up a fading bark after we had gone, until you could have put that sound in a little glass jar, then a thimble, then it was lost in the fabric of neighborhood traffic. Charles was satisfied and swung that cone megaphone towards the next sounds coming our way.

This sidewalk we followed, with houses on our right, the street on our left and more houses on the other side of pavement, was probably once a nice path through the trees not so very long ago. Charles probably knew that. She could probably smell that old world hidden by our years.

Rebecca and I chatted about whatever. Nothing much. I could see where the laundromat would be, on the corner a couple blocks away. Like some radio DJ with a song just long enough to take us there, we made up a story about Charles going to the laundry. She unzipped her yellow fur to have it cleaned. She borrowed a very nice robe and went next door to a coffee shop to wait, but when she returned, the laundromat had lost her coat. That's why they have those tickets, I explained, and they keep everything wrapped on that great hanging conveyor belt. The laundromat owner was shocked, she couldn't understand how it happened. She urged Charles to please accept a fine white polar bear coat instead, but Charles said it was too hot for that. Fortunately, Rebecca added, Charles' sense of smell was amplified by the cone. It was like a radar dish and she could smell for miles. Even if nobody else could see it, Charles knew right where it was. I smiled. I told Rebecca I had just been thinking that too, giving Charles the power to smell through time, to when there were no cars here, or houses or yards, when only animals lived in this place.

"Oh Charles!" Rebecca said and gave that sunny fur a scratch. "What a hero."

Charles wagged her tail and stopped walking beside the chrome trimmed windows of the laundromat like she knew this was our destination. Our story had taken us there.

"Here we are," I said.

"Okay," Rebecca said. She stood on one leg and balanced the briefcase on her knee. "I typed a few copies of this," she said, "just in case." When she got one out, she shut the briefcase again and took a deep breath. She bit her lip and looked at me, "Here I go."

I still have not met her parents and I don't know who they are, but I wish they could have seen her then. She was brave as can be and I saluted her and said, "March right up to that counter fearlessly."

She nodded. Her eyes darted and she followed their direction inside the room full of washing machines. I could see her cross the floor, but I didn't dare watch any more. For now she was on her own. There were plenty of flyers and notices taped to the window and I turned my attention to them. Guitar lessons, a room for rent, a bicycle for sale. The 4 Peters, the teen band, was coming to town. They're all the rage among the young and even the ones who visit our house know them. Right beside the door was a handwritten note that I just barely had time to read:

> To whom ever is
> trying to pick the locks
> on my machines, even if
> you succeed you can't get
> much. All machines are emptied
> at 700 PM
> I now have <u>the police</u>
> <u>driving</u> by at <u>night</u>

"Never mind," Rebecca said. She was back at my side already. "Let's go."

"What happened?"

"Never mind," she repeated. She looked stricken. She looked totally different than she had going in.

"What happened?"

"Nothing!" she stamped her foot, "Please can we go?"

Charles and I had to catch up with her.

I stayed silent. I could hear Charles panting breath out the cone.

As we crossed the street, she explained,

"They didn't want me." The hand clutching her resume tightened to a fist, bending the paper into sharp corners. She sighed loudly, "I knew it! I knew I shouldn't have gone in there."

Rebecca was ready to storm right back home the way we had come, but I turned Charles on the next corner. "Hold on," I said. "I know a place you'll like."

"I want to go to my room," she said. It was a terrible sight to see her now, to hear the hurt, and the tears building in her eyes.

"We will," I said. "This is on the way."

She stood there with that briefcase and crumpled parchment and she looked like she was done with the world.

"You'll like it," I promised again.

Her green dress only made her seem limp as celery now. She let go of a shipwrecked sigh. "What is it?"

I pointed down the block, the row of trees and parked cars, the awnings throwing shade on the sidewalk. With my fingertip, I touched the spot down the street where I knew she could start over again.

6.
ALONE

We stood on the sidewalk and finished our lemonades. Beside us was the wooden pushcart. Chopped lemons floated like goldfish in a big glass tank.

After a minute or so, she apologized.

I said, "What for?"

"I thought I could get a job there."

I said, "I know you're disappointed, but I'm glad you didn't. You should have seen the sign on the window." I took a sip of lemonade and told her about it.

She stared at me, wide-eyed, "Someone's stealing from the machines?"

"Picking the locks! Like a fiendish master criminal on the loose!"

That got her to laugh.

"And despite the best efforts of the nightly police patrol, The Washing Machine Thief arrives and disappears, always leaving their calling card…"

"Yes," she said in a sinister voice, "A single argyle sock."

We laughed at that absurd thought. She was good at this game, making up stories that flickered in your mind like movies. It was too bad I couldn't put her in my book and pay her royalties. But she was more than a chapter set in this small window of time—she deserved adventures big as a library. I finished my lemonade. Charles tugged at her leash. It was dusk.

The book shop behind us was closing for the day. The owner was moving cardboard boxes inside. There were so many books they spilled out onto the sidewalk.

"Hi," I said. I knew him a little bit. Not well enough to know his name or his story. I knew him by the way he had turned reality into this shop full of great books and always good music playing, providing a place in the world you could drift into like a dream. Sometimes I would just stand next to a bookshelf and stare out the window and watch the bay.

"How are you?" he mumbled.

"We're better now," I said. "My friend Rebecca here is looking for a job. Are you hiring?"

He gave her a look, a book settling in the crook of his arm. "Do you have any experience working in a bookstore?"

"No," Rebecca sighed. "But I read a lot."

He smiled slowly and said, "That counts."

"I have my resume," Rebecca said. She set her briefcase down and used both hands to straighten the paper.

He nodded as he looked it over. "You're a good typist too," he said and, "Sometimes I need help with inventory."

"Oh!" she said. You could have put feathers on that word and flown it to the moon.

"It's not a regular job," he continued. "But I can give you a call and see if you're still interested."

Rebecca said, "Thank you so much."

"Alright," he replied. For all those books, he wasn't the wordiest person. He nodded to us and carried another box inside.

Whatever electricity it is that teenagers run on, Rebecca was fluttering now and happy again as we walked towards home. I was walking with green spring again.

"My parents have been bugging me to get a job," she said. "A job and then it will be a place of my own. Ugh! One step at a time, I guess." She swung the briefcase in her hand like a pendulum. "Thanks for taking me down that street."

"Well, I wasn't expecting that to happen. That just goes to show, you never know what will happen. Even when it looked bleak as can be, we stopped for lemonade and turned the tide." Sometimes it seems like we're moving along in a strange machine and if you feed it black coal that's the cloud you'll be traveling in. What we did was hoist up a lemonade sail and the wind took us somewhere else.

Charles pulled my arm towards the yard with the picket fence. I forgot about that barking little dog, but Charles hadn't. Her cone swiveled, searching for him. "Sorry, Charlie," I said. "Looks like Rudolph must have gone inside."

"Rudolph?"

"I call that little dog Rudolph Valentino. He and Charles are tragically in love—this fence always keeps them apart."

watching the whole thing

"Oh, poor Charles," Rebecca cooed and gave her a pat.

"I know," I said. "Even Shakespeare is moved." I pointed at the tall cedar tree on the edge of their yard. "He's up there hiding in the branches, watching the whole thing."

"I see him…" Rebecca whispered. "He's writing it all down. With a quill pen."

We weren't surprised as the top of the tree gave a little nod either from the wind or the weight of that famous bard.

"Do you think we better call the fire department to get Shakespeare down?"

"I think they only do that for cats," Rebecca said. "Besides, he might not want to come down. He would have to go out looking for a job too."

I laughed. But she was right, and it made me wonder where Shakespeare would end up in today's world. I'd let him work with me at the cemetery. I'd get him his own typewriter.

Charles wasn't concerned. She only had one more sniff for the air fenced in there and then she led the way again.

Rebecca had got quiet again. She stared

at the passing flowers and asked me, "Do you ever have job openings at the cemetery?"

"For Shakespeare?"

"No, for me."

"Rebecca, you don't want to work there. That's the end of the line. You're—"

"Oh no!" she interrupted me. She was staring down the length of sidewalk, but all I could see was our neighborhood, the trees framing the roof of our house and a purple-turning sky.

"What is it?"

"That's my parent's car! It's parked across the street."

"Well," I started to say, "They're probably—"

"No! I'm not ready to go!"

She was falling back into her panic mode faster than I could hope to catch. Before I could react, she was running towards them. Charles and I stood in place watching a firework rocket hiss off the ground, knowing there would be a bang.

"Come on Charles," I said. "We better see what we can do."

The car doors opened and I could already hear the commotion. Rebecca, that sweet girl from a moment ago, was shouting and waving her arms in the street. Fortunately, I could also see Angie heading out there to ward off a riot.

I gave Charles a pat on the shoulder. It was time for her to turn into a Saint Bernard and dig into the avalanche.

The air was bristling around that parked car. It was a shock hearing the screaming and cussing coming from Rebecca. I was surprised all the flowers hadn't jumped out of the ground and gone running.

Angie had planted herself between Rebecca and her mother and was working to soothe them. It wouldn't be long.

"I'm not going!" Rebecca stomped her foot.

It wouldn't be too long.

I've seen my wife work her magic many times before. It was already working. She knew just what to say and how to get a fire under control. There wasn't much I could do but stand on the sidewalk shore and wait for shipwreck survivors. With a weary groan,

Charles lay down on the strip of grass.

I don't know if he just appeared or if he had been waiting in the same spot too, but a man next to me struck a match to a cigarette and asked, "Is this what anyone wants?" The smoke from him breezed. "We're trying to tell her about responsibilities. She won't listen. How's she going to survive if she can't support herself with a job? She won't even learn how to cook." He inhaled more smoke and spoke again, "I don't know how we ended up here. You start out devoting your life to this person, the whole wonder of falling in love with some-one. You want to give them the world. Then if you have a child, that love goes into them, the love that you used to share. You start feeling it less and tensions start occurring. You've got to work a lot more for a family. Resentments and misunderstandings start cropping up. Life is so different than the days running around with that person you fell in love with, the girl I used to know."

It could have been a common speech he gave to any man who would listen, but his wife must have heard that, or sensed his words, and

I wasn't surprised when she looked at him and rolled her eyes. She gave her daughter a hug and a kiss and Rebecca walked our way with Angie's arm around her shoulders.

"Anyway," Rebecca's peculiar father said to me, to the stage and audience before him, "Thanks to you, it looks like we'll get another night alone."

7.
FAILURE

I can't claim to understand it all. That's the problem with this kind of book I'm writing. I'm supposed to come off as some sort of expert and all these words are supposed to work as some kind of magic spell. Honestly, I don't know if they will. I can't make any promises.

Is this the time to admit to my own failure? I know it's important. If you want to understand The Orphanage of Abandoned Teenagers, it really lies at the heart…No, I don't think I'm ready to talk about it yet.

Rebecca's parents drove off. I do know what they're feeling—parents could use their own orphanage from time to time too—a place they can escape to, away from the pressures and drama. After all, they're going through just as much change as their child.

I was glad Rebecca was still with us. Our walk had been fun. She was smart, sweet and interesting, and despite her outburst, she really was getting ready for the world. But her recent street performance seemed to have worn her out. With her parents gone, she curled up on the couch, sipped the tea my wife made, and wrote in her journal. Charles lay at her feet, head disappeared in her cone like a sleeping hermit crab.

Angie read her book, music played softly, I was staring at the crossword puzzle, when there was a knock on the front door.

Charles twitched, barked, lifted her funnel and I shot Angie a glance.

"I'll see who it is," she said.

Rebecca looked at me.

"Another arrival at the orphanage," I told her in a horrible *Oliver Twist* accent.

She smiled and we listened through the wall, down the hall.

In a moment, we heard Angie call, "Leo! It's for you!"

"What?" I couldn't imagine. I folded the newspaper and left it on my chair.

At this hour, I didn't know who to expect—Martians, the F.B.I?

It was somewhere in between. Angie stood in the hall beside Count Misfit. He had a suitcase in his hand and he wore the green makeup and his shabby, regal costume.

"I'll go sit with Rebecca," Angie told me.

I was a little surprised by his appearance, but I had a feeling what would be next.

"Leo," he said, "I'm sorry for the intrusion. I'm out of sorts. My girlfriend kicked me out and I have nowhere to go. I'm distraught."

"You're welcome to stay here," I said.

"Just a couple nights, just until I get back on my feet?"

"Sure." Sure, why not have The Count here too? He wasn't that different than our orphans. In most ways he stayed planted in that fantasyland, second star to the right, and straight on till morning.

"Crowning achievement!" He bowed, reached out and shook my hand. He was in royal character. How could I refuse The Count? "I'll remember you when my ship comes in." He gave his suitcase a shake. "Can I leave this meager collection of my worldly goods?"

"Of course."

He set it on the floor and with a sweep of his hand checked the watch in his topcoat pocket. It was attached by a thick silver chain.

I've seen him do the same thing on TV a hundred times, when he would announce, "And now it's time for a commercial." He took a look at the saucer-sized clock face and gave a White Rabbit cry of alarm. "Alas, I must hurry. The program awaits."

"Okay," I said. "We'll see you later tonight then."

He bowed again.

"Oh," I remembered to ask before he left, "What film are you showing?"

"An appropriate one to be sure. Do you recall *The Mummy's Curse*?"

"I think I do."

"Then it's up to you to reacquaint yourself with it. I'll see you later." He shut the door and for a moment I could see him in the window, cape billowing as he hurried towards his car.

I do wonder what people think as they're driving along in the moonlight and neon and they happen to glance at the car pulling up next to them and the driver is a green ghoul in a top hat and cape. I love it. It's just like I tell our visitors at the orphanage when they're head bowed down and stuck in a rut—look up, look around, you never know what to expect.

And he has the same effect on the TV too—it's really sort of a miracle The Count is even there—amid the commercials, all the throwaway products and American noise, gloss and sheen—there he is, on a cardboard set, showing eighty year old movies, weird black and white dreams he has swept out of the shadows. I love it.

When I returned to our room with the moth-like Ray Noble Orchestra, comfortable chairs, a pot of tea and my crossword puzzle, I was thinking about Lon Chaney's monster, sitting there with us in his rags and Egyptian dust and endlessly searching heart.

"Let me guess," Angie said, "Is The Count spending the night?"

"I hope that's okay. He's temporarily homeless."

My wife nodded and Rebecca asked, "Who's The Count?"

"Count Misfit," Angie began. "Leo, where do we start?"

It was a good question. I've known him a

long time. I sat down. "Well, first of all, I work with him at the cemetery. His real job though happens at night. He has a show on TV where he invites old movies over."

Angie laughed. "He's also bright green."

Rebecca stared. "What?"

"He's not the sort of person you meet every day," I told Rebecca. "Well, *I* do. I like to think of him as a sort of time traveler from a lost age of castles and forests and ghosts on dark roads."

"And he'll be sleeping upstairs from you, Rebecca!" Angie said and they laughed.

I returned my attention to my crossword. There wasn't much I could do with it. I imagined a millipede crawling around a maze. It wasn't getting anywhere. I was stuck for the moment. The last word I had written was Oleo. "I'm going to wait for his show to come on," I said at last.

I left my chair. I had given up on the crossword. Maybe some clever forgotten man like William Powell would find it in the ash at the city dump and fill in the blank spaces for me. That was my hope for it anyway.

Along the wall, underneath a painting of the sea, we have a gigantic old wooden TV cabinet. It's the grandfather clock of televisions. It was here when we moved into the house, like one of those boats people make in a basement and discover that it can't fit out the door when it's done. A long history of America had shown on its screen. I turned a switch and it would take a moment to breathe back into life. There was a tiny star-sized dot of blue light that slowly grew.

What a pretty strange and amazing machine when you think about it. You turn it on and you never know where you will be— in someone else's house, a car lot, a jungle, another planet. This time it was a commercial for coffee. A couple walked along a beach at sunrise and as the jingle played, a cup filled with coffee in the sky. "It must be just about time," I said.

There was another ad though. This one with a loud clown running back and forth. I touched the dial and turned the sound down. The bright tint of the TV made him glow like a comet.

"What movie is he hosting tonight?" Angie said.

"*The Mummy's Curse.*"

"Oooh!" they both cooed.

Just then the screen went blue as a swimming pool, and then an announcement in white letters appeared. I turned up the sound.

"The following is a paid program and does not necessarily represent the views and opinions held by the staff and management of this station."

I barely had time to think about what just happened, when the phone began to ring.

"What happened to his show?" said Rebecca.

I said, "I don't know. I'll be right back," as I hurried out of the room. I was sure it was The Count on the phone.

There's an old telephone on the wall in the hall, the same one installed when this was a boarding house. It gave one more insistent ring before I yanked the receiver free. "Hello?" I said.

"It's me," The Count said miserably. All the sand had run out of the castle. He took a deep breath and sighed, "They canceled my show."

8.
MYSTERY

The Count never showed up at the orphanage. It was Saturday morning. We talked about it at the table. He had gone missing. So it was up to me to become a detective.

He didn't answer the phone at the cemetery. I didn't know the telephone number at his girlfriend's house, but I knew where she lived. I drove him there sometimes. Even though she kicked him out, she might know his whereabouts.

After breakfast, Rebecca asked if she could help me look for him. I didn't mind the company. Angie thought it would be fine. She gave us a list of groceries.

Then, as we were leaving Angie stopped us in the driveway. "Take a resume along with you." She passed it to Rebecca, who sighed a little. "You never know," Angie said.

"I know," said Rebecca. "Thanks."

"Don't get involved in some big mystery!" Angie called after us, as I opened the car door for Rebecca. "Try to be home by lunch."

"Who knows?" I told her, "This is just the beginning of The Search for Count Misfit." I gave a laugh like one of those movie mad scientists. I waved, got in the car, and shut the door.

The engine started right up and the radio came on. It was static. Before we could go, we needed music.

"Where do we start?" Rebecca said.

"Ummm…" I was distracted by dialing sound, voices and noise. My favorite spot is the pirate radio station, but you really have to search for it. The frequency moves around as much as their location. One day they're up on the roof of someone's house in the Southside and the next day they're broadcasting from a tree at Roosevelt Park.

"Should we start at the TV station?" Rebecca asked.

A warbling song arrived on the airwaves. "Ahah!" I grinned at her and put the car in gear. The road was clear, I tapped my fingers on the steering wheel. I imparted some valuable advice about driving with music.

We turned the corner and pointed towards downtown, the tall old stone buildings and the cement factory smokestack. We passed a row of cottonwood, but they weren't snowing today.

Thin as a needle, I could see the tall KGUS antenna on the skyline. "Do you think we should start at the TV station?" I asked.

"That's what I said!" Rebecca poked me in the arm, "That's what I said before we left!"

"Yes, of course. And you were right on the money." We came to a stop and waited for the traffic light to change. "If we're lucky, The Count told someone there something." The light turned green and we were on our way. "But knowing The Count, he probably just disappeared into the night."

"Hmm," said Rebecca. "You think he's been wandering the streets ever since?"

A lot of people do. If you can imagine an invisible river we float back and forth in. It was a big enough town he could stay lost a while if he wanted to. "I don't know. I hope not…" I wondered if there was a hole in the cement, maybe down the next street, where he might have hid. That's what the monsters in those late night movies did. And somehow they always came back from defeat.

I don't understand why people wanting to do their heart's desire can't. I really believe people are put here to do the thing inside of them, that makes their life the happiest, that make their lifetime complete. You wouldn't grow flowers if you didn't want them to bloom. I know it's funny to think of Count Misfit's show as some strange garden but that's what it is. I see him doing exactly what he's meant to do at this time on planet Earth.

Rebecca turned in her seat. She stared at the windows of the diner on the corner. Then she gave a laugh. "I don't even know what Count Misfit looks like! I'm just looking for someone who's green."

"Right. Well, chances are if you do see someone green, that's him. Add a cape and a top hat and it's pretty much a guarantee."

With a smile, she kept watching out the window while the radio played its next song and we rolled up to the curb beside KGUS.

I was surprised to see a big red and white sign planted by the front door—For Sale. I stared through the windshield and sighed, "Oh no…"

Rebecca said, "I think we found our first clue."

"Yeah."

"What do we do now?"

I took the keys out of the ignition and held them tight in my hand. "We go see if there's anyone left." I opened the door and I felt like on old movie cowboy staring at the remains of Fort Apache.

Rebecca came around from the other side of the car and we followed the sidewalk. The big windows were coated in something reflective and silver and you couldn't really tell if there were lights on in there.

Angie and I came here once a few years back for a Halloween party that The Count was throwing for his show. There were a lot of the local luminaries invited—morticians, cooks and waitresses, some librarians and poets, a car dealer, ballet dancers, even a scout troop. That was quite a crowd that night.

The door had a big gold number 12

painted on the glass. I took hold of the handle and opened it for Rebecca. What would happen to Channel 12? Had it sent its last beams of light out into the universe?

We walked into a carpeted lobby and a woman looked up at us from paperwork piled on her desk. She had the frantic expression of a sailor watching for sharks. Around her feet, cardboard boxes were set on the floor like stepping stones marched down the hallway. If there was one big enough for Count Misfit, I would have looked inside.

I said, "Hello," and gave a little wave in hopes her stricken look would fade.

It did. For a second anyway she looked much relieved. "You're not from Accounting?"

Did it look like I was? Did Accounting arrive looking this way, in worn-out clothes and worried, with a teenage girl for muscle? "Accounting? No, we're just looking for a friend of mine who works here. Or worked here—past tense."

"Oh," she said. She pushed her glasses. "Nobody's working here anymore. Not even me. I was sent here by the temp agency. I have to get all these files put in order. I don't know how to make labels though. I have no idea how this machine works!" She pointed fearfully at the big electric typewriter.

Fortunately, my partner did. Rebecca left me and went around the desk, avoiding boxes and spilled paper. "I can help you with that."

"Can you, dear?"

Rebecca felt beneath the corner of the typewriter and switched it on. The platen made a loud clunk and the secretary pivoted backwards in fright. "It's okay," Rebecca said. "Now it's ready to go." She picked up a thin cardboard box, "These are the labels?"

"Yes."

"And it looks like this is the list that needs to be typed…" Rebecca leafed through the stapled packet. "Wow. There's a lot."

"I know!"

I just stood there, impressed by Rebecca as she took a sheet of label paper and fed it into the machine and talked to the poor lady so she could see it wasn't an impossibility.

She laughed and told Rebecca, "You

saved my day. I think I can do this now." The typewriter hummed like a tractor.

Rebecca stood beside me again and I gave her shoulder a squeeze. She made a difference in the world.

The temp said, "I wish I could help you find your friend, but I haven't seen anyone since the guard let me in this morning. This place is like a ghost town."

I nodded. I didn't want to keep her from her job. "Okay. Thanks."

"Thank you," she said. "Especially the young lady. I don't know where I'd be without you."

Shy, Rebecca sort of ducked and rolled her eyes, and it made me smile to see her smile. We felt good about leaving the ruined station, until we were back outside and realized we weren't a step closer to finding Count Misfit.

9.
TEMPORARY

There was no reply at his girlfriend's apartment. The intercom buzzed, but she wasn't there apparently. We looked up the stone wall of the four story building and I pointed out her window. It looked like all the others, touched by the sunlight of a late morning.

We got back in the car and drove to the Bayview Cemetery. That was the only other place I could think of. I should have asked Rebecca for her ideas—it would have saved some time.

The pirate radio had already moved, leaving only a dull static where it had been earlier. But Rebecca was able to dial it in again. I told her about the time Count Misfit was invited on the air. Sometimes they have guests who can enchant you with things you never knew. That day he was scheduled, The Count couldn't start his car, so I drove him. He got the station directions only an hour before. It didn't seem possible—we were in the midst of a neighborhood, houses crowded together with trees and gardens—and as he read from the crumpled handwritten note, he suddenly said, "Stop! That's it!" Actually, it was the perfect disguise. A narrow brick colored house, half-hidden by shrubs. We pulled into a driveway just snug enough to fit the car. The Count took me to a wooden gate that led to the backyard. That's where we spent the next hour, in a tent, while a twelve year old boy asked The Count all about strange movie worlds.

Rebecca listened, but I could tell there was something else on her mind, past these rooftops and trees, something that hung like a kite in the air. We were close to the cemetery when she finally asked me, "What's a temp agency? That lady at the TV station said she was sent by the temp agency."

"Oh boy. A temp agency is a place that hires out people for temporary placement in jobs. I've had my share doing that kind of work. They place you in factories or offices, construction sites, that sort of thing. Usually the job only lasts a day, a couple days, or a week. Back when I was starting out, I thought, oh, as someone who wants to be a writer, I should experience as many kinds of jobs as possible. That's the reality of America, right? That will give me all sorts of inspiration to write about."

"Did it?"

"Sure, I suppose. But so does everything being alive." I laughed, "And now, here we are at the cemetery."

It was true.

"Do you think I should get a temp job?" she asked.

I shrugged. "At this point in your life, a lot of the jobs out there for you are pretty pointless really, but they get you out into the world, they let you be a part of it. That's the big thing—you see that you make a difference. Even if it's serving ice cream."

I parked the car in its usual spot. The Count's car wasn't to be seen. I wished I would have looked for it at the TV station lot. It could have been behind the building. That could have been a valuable clue. I thought of telling Rebecca, but I didn't want to look like a total amateur. I liked pretending I knew what I was doing, that I was a sort of Columbo or Rockford, with an end in sight.

Rebecca stood next to the car and surveyed the green field full of stones. "Wow," she said. "I've never been to a cemetery before."

I was glad for that, in spite of the way she looked around so wondrously.

She fluttered along with me to the office. It wasn't open today and there was no coffee aroma standing guard at the door. I was sure that if The Count was taking refuge here, the coffee would let me know.

Inside was that green gloom allowed by the narrow window. It was very quiet, until Rebecca saw the old wooden telephone booth and gasped.

"I love it!" she said and rushed towards it. A lot of people coming here have that reaction—it looks like it belonged in a carnival sideshow or some ghost town bus station, and who knows, maybe at one time it did?

She heaved open the door and stepped inside. She sat on the wooden chair and put her hand on the heavy black receiver attached to the wall.

"I would be careful of that if I were you," I told her. "People say that phone connects you to the land of the dead."

"What?"

"But since you've come this far, what's to stop you from giving it a listen?" I tried my best to make what I said seem real, and she watched me closely, waiting for me to break. Maybe if she was a little younger, maybe if I was more convincing, but she wanted to believe.

She picked up the phone and brought it to her ear. Her eyes wandered to the dark eaves of the phone booth interior as if a moth up there had caught her attention. Then all of a sudden she said, "Yes, hello operator. Could you tell me if Count Misfit is there? We've been looking for him all morning. We hope nothing bad happened to him." Rebecca paused, as if she was genuinely listening to some ghostly switchboard voice. She smiled and I couldn't help smiling too as she replied, "Oh, that *is* good news. Thank you. Goodbye."

She replaced the phone on its cradle and emerged from that shadowy wooden box. "Everything's going to be alright. They don't have anyone named Count Misfit there."

And I was so relieved.

Even though I know that phone hasn't worked in years.

10.
WATERMELON

So we went back home. We did as much as we could. It was lunchtime and we were hungry. Of course once we were there in the kitchen, looking for food, Angie asked if we had been to the store. The grocery list was still crumpled in my pocket!

After a couple sandwiches, Rebecca and I hit the road again. Like I said before, it was fun having her along, even though as crime-solving partners we were less than successful. Now we had a new undertaking. Food Giant wasn't far away.

It was right where it had always been. No dark force could tear it out of the ground and hide it behind the streets and cement walls of the city like a fairytale sufferer, or like Count Misfit gone with the wind.

Rebecca was in a chatty good mood. We drove along with the radio on and I imagined her voice as one of the instruments in the orchestra, some rare woodwind that played amid the string section the way lake weed will flow in the current.

The big metal letters of Food Giant appeared on the next corner. High above the parking lot they popped with red neon bulbs. I saw a pigeon start to land on one, then change its mind.

"Oh! I love this store!" Rebecca told me.

I come here just about every time I shop for food and I feel the same way too, though she is more radiant about it. It's one of those strange and wonderful examples of living in this age, where what you need is waiting for you all wrapped in bright electricity. I've learned to be thankful of marvels, but it's always good to be remind-ed. All it takes is something foolish for that to snap—a war, a bomb, a team of bulldozers with blueprints for a bigger parking lot. We're lucky. We need to be thankful. And nothing said it better than her hopping out of the car and holding her hands out to the miraculous neon appearance.

I couldn't help but like Rebecca. Even as I caught up with her (and for a split moment recalled the way she had acted yesterday when

what you need is waiting

her parents arrived) I knew that Rebecca was going to be fine out in the big world.

As we crossed the parking lot, I removed the shopping list from my pocket. There weren't too many items on it, but I told Rebecca, "I can't believe we don't have watermelon on here."

"I love watermelon!"

"Me too." I pointed at the wooden bin outside the entrance. "There's no such thing as summer without watermelon."

"Can I pick one?"

"Please." As she hurried to their corral, I pulled a shopping cart free and rolled it to her.

"Don't you love the feel of these?"

I docked the rattling buggy against the bin. It was filled with the smooth green fruit. Another one of life's miracles. Actually, you could make a list a mile long of miracles.

She was tapping them gently. "Is there a secret to picking the best one?"

"Oh, probably. I think the best way is letting the watermelon find you." I ran my hands over them. "One of them will speak to you." With tapping fingers, I drummed the rind of one while she closed her eyes and divined.

"Here!" She pulled a watermelon free from the crowd. "This is the one." She carried it to the cart, "It's heavy!" She set it in the child's seat and that reminded me of a story from Japan. An old couple open a melon and they find a baby living inside.

"I love it," I said, sounding like her. It's true that these teenagers passing through our lives have their influence on Angie and me. I was admiring the sticker on the shell—it was a cartoon stork delivering a swaddled watermelon—how did they get all these watermelons here? Did they arrive by riverboat from some warm farm far away?—when Rebecca called me.

"Leopold, look!"

She had wandered ahead of me to read a sign taped to one of the store's windows. As I pushed the buggy closer and she stepped aside, I could read it.

Written in thick pen, it said: HELP WANTED.

"Should I get my resume from the car?"

"Sure," I grinned. Rebecca ran onto the pavement and it occurred to me, that's why

Angie wanted us to go shopping. She was clever alright.

The watermelon and I waited for Rebecca, and I remembered many moons ago. When I was a kid, I loved watermelon so much I saved the seeds from each slice I got and I planted them in the alley. I called it an alley, but it was really just an overgrown gap between the neighbor's house and ours. Even though there was little sun in there, the seeds took root and grew. Little green stems, leaves small as ladybugs. I had high hopes for them. Before school started again I felt sure there would be a bountiful crop. I could pull a wagon full of them around the block.

Rebecca returned. She was flapping her typewritten page. "Come on!" she sang excitedly and she sprang ahead. One wheel of my grocery buggy spun crazily as I tried to keep up with her.

Maybe the lunch rush was over, but there were still a fair number of shoppers and I had to slow down to keep from colliding.

Rebecca was fearless. She walked right up to a guy in a tie, the manager I guessed, and I could hear her explain. I didn't want to intrude though, so I stopped by the rack of used paperbacks. I looked at the covers and spun the shelf slowly. It made a fantastic ancient creaking as it turned, as if every one of those books—science fiction, western, fantasy, detective and romance—were hooked to some primeval storytelling machine.

Rebecca and the Food Giant man were still talking, but I tried not to eavesdrop as I kept that medieval contraption in motion. Beyond them, around them, washed all the sounds of the supermarket: register bells and drawers clacking, paper bags crackling, thumping, the murmured radio of voices, the music of speakers hidden in the ceiling, and me contributing too, with that Rumpelstiltskin spinning wheel full of books.

I must admit, every time we come to Food Giant I check this creaky carrousel in hopes that one of my books found its way to this prestigious spot. But so far, no luck. Of course, I could plant one here. Why not?

I stopped turning and daydreaming when Rebecca grabbed my arm. Her eyes sparkled and she smiled, "I got the job."

"Really?"

"Just like that!"

I held out my hand and grinned, "We have to go tell Angie."

"Yes!" she laughed.

We were so excited in our hurry to the car, we left the watermelon behind and all the other groceries we were sent to find too.

11.
HELLOS & GOODBYES

What a day! I was sitting in my chair holding the crossword book when the doorbell rang.

"It's them!" Rebecca called. "Can you let them in, Leopold?" She was lighting candles on the table.

I stood. From the kitchen came the clatter of dishes and Rebecca rushed past me on her way there. I could smell something delicious. Rebecca's parents were in for a surprise—she had a job and she made dinner. I remembered her father on the street yesterday, as I went down the hall and opened the door.

Yesterday was like another planet. They were a family again, sitting at the table, laughing and listening to Rebecca's stories, amazed, proud and smiling with love. They were together again and I know that's great, that's what we all wanted to see happen, but there's also a part to this I don't like—she would be leaving and I was missing her already.

I excused myself and stood up, "I'll be

right back." Her father barely broke the beat in his story, one of those memories the three of them shared and knew like a myth.

I went out to the hallway and leaned on the stairway railing.

It's the nature of our orphanage that these kids come and go. There's an endless tide of them. Tonight there will probably be a knock on the door and we'll start over again.

Angie crept up behind me and put her arms around me. "You okay?" she said.

"Oh, I'm fine."

Rebecca laughed from the other room.

Angie and I have been through this before. Sometimes you get close to one, you almost think they're yours.

Angie rubbed my shoulder. "She's very happy now."

"I know." I let go of the bannister and looked at the floor. "Hey," I turned and asked her, "What happened to The Count's suitcase? He left it here."

"I moved it upstairs, to his room."

I said, "Oh."

"I hope he shows up soon."

"Me too," I said.

She smiled, tugged my sleeve, "We better get back."

"Okay."

It was okay. I did get up from the table one more time, ostensibly to start clearing the dishes, and as I brought the last of them to the kitchen, I stayed in there to run water in the sink. Maybe all these goodbyes were getting to be too much. It doesn't get any easier, and as you get older there seems to be a lot more of them. Hello to someone you really get to like, and then a goodbye and they're out of your life. It was the nature of the orphanage. We were only meant to be in their life for so long anyway, to provide a safe place for support and care.

I let my hands sink into the warm soapy water. It was better to be in here washing dishes, to let her go and float away with water.

Whatever my weird reasoning was, it wasn't long before I was rinsing off a spoon and I heard my name called.

"Leopold." It was Rebecca. She stood in the doorway. "We're going back home now."

She walked into the kitchen. "I wanted to thank you again."

"Yes," I said. "Thank you to you too."

"I'm going to give you a hug."

"Oh yes. That would be nice if you don't mind."

She laughed, "Of course I don't mind." And quick as someone with wings, she had her arms around me.

"I'm going to miss you," I said. What a world.

"Me too."

"And we never got to find Count Misfit."

"I've been thinking about that." She let me go and took a step back and pointed at the ceiling. "I meant to ask you this morning, have you checked the bag he left?"

I smiled and shook my head. "No," I said. "That's a great idea though. I don't know why I didn't think of that earlier."

"That's what partners are for."

I nodded.

"But you have to call me and tell me what you find out. Okay, partner?" She held out her hand.

"Okay," I said and took her hand. "It's a deal."

We shook. She waved and left the kitchen. It was good we weren't done with each other yet. I still had that spoon in my hand and I put it with the others. I could hear Rebecca, her parents and Angie talking in the hall, leaving for the door. What a world.

There was one last sing-song of goodbyes and then the door shut.

It was quiet. It was just Angie and me and Charles in the orphanage. How many times have we had this happen? We keep a book upstairs. It's filled with names. Over half the pages are written on.

I left the pond of dishwater and went into the hallway to see Angie. She held a finger to the curtain, looking out at the street. She waved and her head turned to follow that car out there leaving.

"Hellos and goodbyes," I said. I put my hands on her shoulders.

12.
YOUR FORTUNE

I actually knocked on the door of Count Misfit's room, as if his suitcase needed to know I was entering. It was a strange thing to do, I know.

The door creaked as I pushed it open. Blue in the evening's light, I could see that suitcase laid at the foot of his bed. Of course, this whole thing resembled a scene from one of his movies—*Count Misfit's Suitcase*—all it needed was a bolt of lightning in the window. And just like one of those heroic fools in film, I entered the room.

I reached along the wallpaper and hit the light switch and the lamp beside the bed turned on. It was just a suitcase, I don't know why I was getting myself all worked up. Still, if Rebecca was here, I think I'd have her open it instead of me. Just in case.

I stopped at the bed, and with an arm's length between me and the suitcase, stretched out and flicked the latches. If there was an octopus waiting to spring out, I was tensed and ready to dive for cover. I took a deep breath and flipped the lid open.

Only a worn black typewriter case rested inside, packed safely with socks and some other clothing pushed around it. Anyone who hasn't seen The Count Misfit Show probably wouldn't know what it was. But I knew. Also, it was painted in pale green letters on the lid: The Talking Hand.

Every once in a while The Count will pull that box off the cobwebbed shelf and open it. He says something that relates to the movie, funny or ironic, then he might ask the Hand, "What should Peter Lorre do?" And then, for all of us viewers, we would watch as the Hand crawled across the keys of its typewriter. It was a little eerie, but you can do just about anything with special effects. It really did look real, but maybe it was just a puppet, or some stagehand reaching up from below.

I opened the typewriter case and sure enough, there was The Talking Hand. It was pale and resting on the keys like a sleeping spider.

Anytime that Peter Lorre, Lon Chaney,

Myrna Loy or any other movie hero was in trouble, the Hand always gave an answer. All I had to do was ask.

I cleared my throat and gave it a try. "Where can I find Count Misfit?"

I waited for the Hand to jump. I knew it would. I waited a couple more seconds and then I jumped when it did, slamming the lid of the suitcase shut.

I'll admit it was cowardly. I confess I must have leaped a foot back from the bed.

The same thing happened when I was about twelve. I was spending the night at a friend's and there was a ghost walking around in the room. You would think I would have realized what a rare opportunity that was. Maybe the ghost could have told me an amazing story about the next world. Instead, I did the same thing I did now—I didn't stop until I was on the other side of the door.

Only when I was in the hall could I catch my breath and think about what I'd seen. Was The Talking Hand really alive? It moved! But that didn't mean it was a living thing, right? Maybe it was just a clever machine. It did look like something you'd see at a circus sideshow. You feed it a dime and it moves and types your random fortune. I knew it had to be that, but I didn't want to go back in the room and check. It could wait until tomorrow. It was late.

I laughed at myself as I walked down the hallway. It's amazing how superstitious you can get if you're not careful.

13.
HOMELESS

In the morning, I took Charles for a walk. I didn't tell Angie about the trick hand. Anyway, she might have known about it already. She carried The Count's bag up to the room. Knowing her, she probably couldn't resist looking in. It was the old Pandora's Box story. But if she did look, she didn't let on. Maybe she felt the same way about it that I did—like some rube jumping at shadows. I guess it made for a pretty funny story though.

I gave Charles' leash a tug as she spent a little too long sniffing the marker post at the start of the trail.

You can't take yourself too seriously. Besides, it would be worth it to see Angie laugh when I told her what happened to me last night.

Just two blocks from our house, the neighborhood turns back into the trees it used to be. I unleashed Charles and let her hurry ahead of me on the trail. Actually, you can see signs of where this used to be farmland fifty years ago or so. There's a couple old fence posts with barbed wire tangled in overgrowth. A few of the fruit trees, apple, pear, plum, still grow among the alder, fir and cedar. The smell of ripe blackberries was tart in the air. Charles stopped at the first thicket we came to and brushed her cone against the thorns. Like some weirdly evolved creature, she used that plastic to knock the berries onto the ground where she could vacuum them up. She's got a real sweet tooth. She would probably forage all day if not for me.

"Come on, Charles," I said.

The hawthorn tree above us squeaked with the sound of little birds. Charles didn't pay them any attention, but if a squirrel shook the branch instead, she would crane her neck and bound about. There were rabbits in the woods too—another source of instant Charles excitement.

She trotted along like an astronaut, that great white cone on her head swiveling to catch every smell.

We were lucky to have this other world so close to home. I listened to the birds singing.

I let my thoughts wander and of course they returned to Count Misfit's Talking Hand. For some reason, I just couldn't get around the idea that hand was alive.

I was watching Charles' yellow tail swish back and forth like a paddling oar when the woods behind us crashed. I turned around suddenly and at first I thought it was a bear and her cub jumping out. Something black and heavy thumped onto the path, followed by the leaping shape of a creature I now realized was a man. He was bent all around, swatting at his legs and back. He gave a bestial yell.

"What's the matter?" I called.

He spun and danced around the slumped shape of his backpack on the path.

I put the leash on Charles and as we neared him, I could tell two things. He was one of the homeless who sleep in the woods, and he was jumping about in a cloud of hornets.

The poor man leaped backwards towards us. He slung his coat open and his jeans were slipping off his thin frame. "Are they on me?"

"Yes," I said, "On your coat." They were riveted to it.

He threw it on the ground and as he did, before he spun, I swore I saw what looked like a police badge on the lining of his black jacket. But there were also hornets circling Charles and me.

"Come on!" I told Charles. We ran through the swarming air. "Good luck!" I yelled over my shoulder.

I didn't stop running until we turned a bend and then I knocked a hornet off my sleeve. I shook my clothing. I couldn't see any more on me.

Charles panted and looked at me with her usual happy grin. A couple hornets were trapped in the cone. "Hold on, Charles." The Velcro made a terrible sound as I pulled it apart and shook it out flat like a carpet. Looking over her fur, I spotted another hornet and flicked it off. "Come on."

We ran a little more and stopped again. Charles didn't seem to have a clue what we had gone through. She wagged her tail and let me reattach the cone. We appeared to be free of those hornets. "What was that, Charles?" The woods were quiet again though, the world was calm. "Okay," I took her leash off and said, "Let's go."

Now we were committed to a long morning walk. We usually turned around and went home the same way, but not today. Those hornets made a wall across the way we had come. And what was the story with that police badge? I couldn't be sure that's what it was—everything happened in a blur—but that's really what it looked like he had in his coat. Was he some undercover cop? Was there a branch of officers they would starve and plant in the forest to go undercover among the homeless? That seemed a bit preposterous. Talk about picking the short straw for assignments. "Forbes, you get Park Avenue…Jones, the Fountain District. Denning, you need to lose sixty pounds and live in a tarp in the woods." Ahh, I was probably just seeing things again. Imagination is the occupational hazard of the writer.

A little ahead of me, Charles waited. The woods ended at another marker post and a car passed on the street just beyond. Charles waited for me to put the leash on her again.

"Good dog." I patted her shoulder and said, "Who would have thought the weather report would include a cloud of bees?"

Outside the shade of trees, we stood on the sidewalk and I thought about which way to go. If I took a left, we could follow the roads around the woods. If we went that way we would end up at home.

But we didn't. We crossed the street. Food Giant was only a few more blocks away. All we had to do was follow that crow.

14.
THE MOVIE IN PROGRESS

I know it was Rebecca's first day and she would be learning her new job. I wasn't sure if she would have time to say hi and talk for a second, but I had to tell her about the suitcase in Count Misfit's room. I still considered her my partner in this strange detective mystery. It wasn't over yet.

I could see the big neon letters of Food Giant rising above the sidewalk trees. We were close, but we didn't make it. A memory got in between.

I guess this is the part of the book where I finally tell you what got me and Angie to start the Orphanage of Abandoned Teenagers. This isn't easy.

I was nearly to the corner of the block. The streetlight was red and a little family was crossing the street: a young woman and man, pushing a baby stroller. That might not sound like much to some readers, or to those who can't remember the feel of the plastic stroller handles bumping along. For me though, that sight was as if all the written pages that had gone by fell out of the sky, and I was staring at Angie and me and our new baby. The breath hitched in my throat and my eyes welled with tears and I had to turn my attention away. I was lucky there was a bench for me to sit on. I fell back against those slats while the world swerved. I'm still not very strong about the whole thing—I kept my hands pressed to my eyes to give the family time to walk away.

That plastic cone clunked against me as Charles tried to comfort me, or get me moving again. Then, with a groan, she lay down at my feet.

Sorry it took me so long to mention the child we lost. A better author might have begun with a shock like that. A movie would have faded from that death, to the front door of the orphanage. It just isn't that easy to talk about. And if it's okay with you, I'd rather not say anymore. It took us a long time, Angie and me, to get over it. I guess you never really do. The orphanage helps.

I held the tears back with my hands and waited for the feeling to pass. I tried to think of other things. It wouldn't do to be spotted crying on a street bench, with a dog wearing a comical cone at my feet. That could quickly end up on the front page of *The Herald*.

I took a deep breath and said, "Okay, Charles?"

She got to her feet and I opened my eyes. It was the 21st Century. Time had passed. "We better go home." Charles was fine with that, she was always fine with anything.

We turned from the sparkling lights of Food Giant and followed the sidewalk. I'm sorry I let memories get the better of me. I know I'm not the only one with an empty part of the heart. I get by filling that empty room with those young people who come and go at the orphanage. If Angie and I can help them out, life is a little bit better.

When we crossed the street, I heard my name called. Along the line of shops, Rebecca waved. She hurried and hopped over to us. Charles thumped her tail.

"Hi Rebecca."

"Hi," she grinned. "I'm on my break. I walked over here for a lemonade." She held up her cup.

"Good idea," I said.

"Is Charles taking you for a walk?"

"Yes, I guess so. We're sightseeing."

Charles clunked Rebecca with her cone and leaned against her leg like a cat.

"Charles misses you."

Rebecca laughed. Her shirt was embroidered with the Food Giant logo and she had a nametag pinned on it.

"How's work?" I asked.

"It's going good. Actually I'm on my way back. Can you walk with me?"

"Sure," I said, "Of course."

She was in good spirits and her words poured happily, "I got to sweep up a spill in Aisle 5. Also, I got to spray the vegetables with a hose. Remember we were joking that I would get a job that had to do with water? Well, it happened! I'm just glad it wasn't that laundromat. Oh, and later, Jim is going to take me up to the roof."

"Is that where you keep the flying fish?"

She laughed and nodded. "We're getting an order of Moon Pies tonight."

I pictured a ghostly looking sailing ship from the moon, hovering overhead, lowering barrels roped together. That vision was a great present from Rebecca, something I haven't thought of before.

She took a sip of lemonade and said, "Oh, did Count Misfit show up yet?"

"Still no sign of him. But you know what? I went up to his room last night like you said to do. I opened that suitcase of his."

"What was in it?" she asked, eyes wide.

We were stopped on the corner, waiting for the crossing light. Charles gave the lamppost a sniff. With a voice full of Transylvanian fog, I told her, "The Talking Hand."

"Aaah!" She hopped off the curb as we started across. "What's that?"

"It's a prop from his TV show. He asks it a question and the Hand types out the answer on a typewriter."

"Yikes!"

"Yes," I said. "Yikes is the correct response."

"What did you do?" she said. Then she grabbed my arm, "You asked it where Count

Misfit was!"

I nodded, "Yes I did. And it sprung to life! Rebecca, I was so startled I slammed the lid and ran out of the room."

"You didn't see what it typed?"

"No. I chickened out."

"Leopold! You have to go back. Aren't you curious? Maybe it typed the answer!"

"I know," I mumbled. It was hard to imagine Philip Marlowe running from that sight in fear. Oh well, we were almost to Food Giant anyway, it was only a block away.

"Ask Angie to go with you," Rebecca decided. "There's safety in numbers."

"That's true."

"I want to know what it typed! Can I call you later? There's a phone in the breakroom."

"Sure."

We stopped on the last curb. The grocery store waited for her on the other side. She hopped onto the crosswalk, "Okay," she called back to me, "I'll phone you pretty soon. Good luck!" She waved and turned and hurried to the next sidewalk. Charles and I stood where we were, like a blind man and his dog, watching until the small sight of her disappeared indoors.

15.
FEARLESS

Charles led me down the alley behind our house and I opened the gate to our backyard. Angie looked up from her book and waved. She sat in the sunshine, enjoying the calm between our teenage tenants.

"Hi," I said.

"Hi. Where have you two been?"

"We got chased by bees in the woods so we took the long way home."

"Bees?"

"Actually, they were hornets. Then we ran into Rebecca."

"In the woods?"

"No," I sat in the chair next to Angie and Charles sank between us. "We saw her afterwards. She was on break from her job, having a lemonade."

"How's Rebecca doing there?"

"Good. They made her the new manager."

Angie made a face.

"No, but it sounds like she's having fun.

Charles and I walked her back to the store. We didn't have too long to talk. Have you heard from The Count?"

She shook her head, "The phone hasn't rung today."

"A quiet orphanage," I said.

We only had the birds around us.

"Well," I started, "I did find what might be a clue in The Count's room."

"Really?" The book on her lap was calling her back though. Honestly, she didn't seem too worried about Count Misfit's whereabouts.

"Rebecca thought it would be a good idea if you looked with me. As a second opinion," I added.

Angie smiled and closed her book. "Alright, Nero Wolfe."

We stood up together. Charles was over by the flowers.

"I don't think you need to be so dramatic though," Angie continued as we crossed the lawn towards the porch steps. "He's not a child. He can do what he wants, he doesn't need our permission."

"I know."

"He's got a car. He probably just drove somewhere else, to another friend's or another place. I'm sure you'll see him at work tomorrow."

I held the door open for her. I said, "Probably," and allowed Charles to trot past.

Angie waited for me in the hallway while the dog walked inside, headed for her water bowl in the kitchen.

"What's the clue you found?"

"You won't like it," I told her. I gave her arm a squeeze and whispered, "It's a monkey's paw."

"Oh no, Leo!" she gasped, "We're doomed!"

I laughed and led the way up the creaking stairs. "Actually, that's not far off. You'll see."

We passed the paintings and photos hung like windows on the wallpaper. If this was a haunted house movie, the music would be chilling, warning us that something was about to happen. The door down the hallway waited for us. "It's still not too late to turn around," I told Angie, as I paused with a hand reached out to the doorknob.

"You want me to go screaming back the way we came?"

"I'll be right behind you," I said. "I'll try not to push you out of the way."

Angie laughed. "Open the door, Leo."

"Okay." I touched the icy diamond-shaped handle and turned it open.

I stood in the doorway a moment, feeling the coolness of the room wash past me, until Angie gave me a gentle push forward.

I stared at the suitcase on the bed. It looked like it hadn't moved since last night. But who really knew for sure? The living hand inside could have crawled out the window and hitched a ride to create mayhem somewhere else. Or not...

"Where's the clue?" Angie whispered. I guess she had caught the feeling in the air.

I pointed at it. "There."

A suitcase on a bed.

"Want me to open it?" I asked.

"You opened your friend's suitcase?"

"I had to! I was looking for clues."

She shook her head. "Oh Leo...What

did you find?"

"Open it," I urged her, "Find out."

She's pretty fearless, I've got to admit. She's always been the no-nonsense one. She didn't have any trouble flicking the suitcase latches and opening the lid. I stood where I was, a couple feet from the bed. I already knew what was in there.

"The Talking Hand!" She turned and smiled, "This is the thing from his show!" Even though she's got her nose in a book while the Creature walks among us, or Dracula returns, she watches The Count every Friday night with me. She pushed the socks aside and opened the typewriter case. It was still in there—I could see it around the shape of her. Like one of those big starfish you see at low tide, it clung spread to the keys.

"What did it type?" I asked. A slice of white paper grinned from the roller.

She leaned close. I shut my eyes. That hand could have stroked her neck. "Let's see…"

I kept my eyes shut tightly as she read the words out loud.

"While I nodded, nearly napping,

suddenly there came a tapping."

I opened my eyes, "That's Poe!"

"I know," she said. "But what's that got to do with Count Misfit?"

I was about to say, "Everything!" How could she have watched him all these years and not seen that? In the very midst of speaking, that one word was cut short by the knock on the door downstairs.

We both jumped. Fast, in the electricity seconds that followed, she slammed the lid of the typewriter box while I hurried to her side and clasped the suitcase lid shut. If we let out some malevolent spirit though, it was probably too late.

"That's weird!" Angie said.

"That's Poe," I repeated. I held her hand and squeezed. "And someone's rapping on our chamber door."

The knock came again. It seemed to go right through the bones of the house.

"You better see who it is," I said.

"*Right*," Angie said. "I saw all those Count Misfit movies with you. You think I'm leaving this room alone? We'll go together."

She tugged my hand.

"Of course. I was only joking."

"It's probably just our next orphan," she said.

"Sure. The son of Doctor Jekyll."

We left the room. At least it wasn't midnight. Plenty of sunshine flowed through the window and filled the hall. Who ever heard of a monster walking around on a sunny Sunday afternoon?

Angie clopped down the stairs in front. She waited a second for me to catch up and we approached the blur pebbled on the glass of the front door. Ahhh, what a short sweet sad life it's been.

there you are!

16.
STARTING OVER

You'll have to excuse me—a guidebook about the troubled teenage years certainly shouldn't become a horror story. Besides, the person at the door had passed his teen years long ago.

Angie said, "Aha! There you are!"

And just like that, the mood changed like the chiming of a clock.

Count Misfit held up a hand and greeted us sheepishly.

I said, "Where have you been?"

Angie stepped aside and motioned him in.

"To the very emotional ends of the world," The Count answered me. "It seems that I've lost everything."

Angie said, "Well, we still have your typewriter."

"Your suitcase!" I quickly said, shooting her a look.

"Yes!" Angie said, "I'll go get your suitcase."

She hurried back up the stairs and it was okay I think. It didn't look like The Count noticed we said too much. He stared at the floor.

"You still have your job at the cemetery," I said.

"That doesn't matter. My girlfriend is gone, the TV show is gone. What more does my heart beat for?"

"I know it seems bad." I heard the floorboards creak overhead. "You had me worried though. I looked all over town for you."

He put his hand to the wallpaper as if any second he would collapse. "I've fallen on hard times. I just couldn't return here. I moved back in with my mother."

"What?"

"Just until I get back on my feet," he added.

"But you can stay here, we have rooms."

"No." He waved his hands emphatically. "Those are for the orphans. I must entrust my fortunes will improve shortly."

I looked at the creaking stairs, the sound of Angie's returning with the suitcase. She held it out in front of her at the end of her reach. I don't blame her. It seemed to have a radioactive effect.

The Count was pleased to see it though. He brightened and smiled briefly. "I thank you, dear lady."

Angie smiled back as she handed it off.

"I really don't mean to trouble you any further," he told us. "I should depart."

I tried to say something comforting, but he was one step ahead of my thoughts and out the door again before I could speak. "I'll see you tomorrow," I called after him.

He held his arm up like a wounded bird's wing as he left our yard, landing back on the sidewalk leading to his parked dented car.

"There goes your mystery solved," Angie said.

I stepped back through the doorway and pulled the door closed on The Count's departure. The door clicked shut and the glass showed only a smeared blue of the day outside.

"He looks so different without his green makeup on and that costume," my wife said. "It took me a minute to recognize him."

I didn't feel like talking. I was thinking. It was hard to believe Count Misfit was gone from the world. You have to have seen his show to know the way he came to life in that role, flapping about the set, joking, popping in and out of the movie.

The door to the kitchen bumped and Charles whined. "Oh," Angie said, "Charles has got herself stuck in there," and she hurried down the hallway to the rescue.

It wouldn't be easy, but right then and there I resolved to do what I could to bring him back to life. Yes, he was just like one of the creatures on his show—no matter how fate, or mankind treated them, they would always return.

"Charles," Angie cooed, "Poor Charles," as she opened the kitchen door.

Charles whined and her toenails clicked her out onto the floorboards. She raced towards me and the cone hit me in the leg.

"Good dog," I gasped as she scratched past me and smelled the floor near the door.

"I'm going back outside with my book," Angie called.

"Okay. I'll come out too."

Charles bumped into me again.

"That was The Count," I told our dog. "You missed him, but he'll be back again sometime."

Charles heard Angie leave the kitchen and ran after her. She always had to be where we were and outside was always better.

I went to the other room where I left my crossword puzzle. I also have a novel somewhere. Angie and I could sit in the backyard holding books open like birdhouses to the sun. But I didn't get far before the phone began to ring.

I picked it up and as usual said, "Hello?"

"Leopold. It's Rebecca."

"Hi Rebecca."

"What happened? What did the Hand type?"

"It typed a spell to make Count Misfit appear."

"Did it? Is he back?"

"Sort of. He showed up here, got the Hand and left again."

"Where was he hiding? Didn't we look

113

everywhere?"

"He's staying at his mother's. I never would have guessed."

Rebecca sighed.

"I know," I agreed. "Not the most exciting conclusion to The Search for Count Misfit. That's how it goes sometimes. He's not very happy about it either."

"I wish there was something we could do."

"Me too. Even Angie noticed he just doesn't look the same. It's like he's missing his soul. He'll be okay though. There must be another TV station, or some space he can rent out at night. He can run a projector, or do a puppet show. I don't know. I'll see him at work tomorrow. Maybe he's thought of something already."

"I hope so."

"What's new at Food Giant? You get onto the roof yet?"

"No," she laughed. "I've been running all over the place, learning everything. It's fun."

"That's good. I'm glad you like what you're doing."

"Well, it's not like being detectives."

"No," I agreed with her.

"I don't want to stop," she quickly said.

"You don't have to. You'll see there are always other mysteries, Rebecca. There's probably one waiting for you right now. Maybe in Aisle 3."

I could hear her sigh on the other end of the line.

I knew she was on her way to another world without me. So was Count Misfit possibly. And whoever came to the orphanage next would make the same journey. Angie and I were here to help them through. This is how it happens. Once they get their wings, they leave.

"Oh," she waited a second. I could see her looking at the white clock face on the wall, or someone waving her back to work. She was already floating away. "I better go."

"Thanks, Rebecca." I knew she wouldn't need the orphanage again.

"You too," she said distantly. "I mean, goodbye."

"Bye."

Weren't there things I wanted to tell

her? As I've said before I'm not that good at this part. I wish there *was* a book that made it easier. I wish I could write it. I've tried.

When I hung up, I sighed. I could feel her thoughts and my thoughts scattered in the air. Now that Count Misfit was cancelled were all our transmissions scrambled? Was his show the glue holding the airwaves together, making sense of monsters and mysteries in the dark? Was this the end of the strange and marvelous? Had some diabolical machine pulled our dreams out of the night? Would anything take their place?

The doorbell chimed.

That sound cleared my mind instantly. I left all my thoughts behind as I returned to the hall. I could see the shapes of them in the glass of the door: the parents and the orphan waiting to come in.

The ORPHANAGE of ABANDONED TEENAGERS

written

May 31, 2016 6:35 AM—September 17, 2016 9:05 AM

Books by Allen Frost

Ohio Trio (Bottom Dog Press 2001)

Bowl of Water (Bottom Dog Press 2003)

Another Life (Bird Dog Publishing 2007)

Home Recordings (Bird Dog Publishing 2009)

The Mermaid Translation (Bird Dog 2010)

The Selected Correspondence of Kenneth Patchen

    edited by Allen Frost (Bottom Dog 2012)

The Wonderful Stupid Man (Bird Dog 2012)

Saint Lemonade (Good Deed Rain 2014)

Playground (Good Deed Rain 2014)

Roosevelt (Good Deed Rain 2015)

5 Novels (Good Deed Rain 2015)

The Sylvan Moore Show (Good Deed Rain 2015)

Town in a Cloud (Good Deed Rain 2015)

At the Edge of America (Good Deed Rain 2016)

Lake Erie Submarine (Good Deed Rain 2016)

The Book of Ticks (Good Deed Rain 2017)

I Can Only Imagine (Good Deed Rain 2017)

The Orphange of Abandoned Teenagers

   (Good Deed Rain 2017)

Also published by Good Deed Rain

A Flutter of Birds Passing Through Heaven:
  A Tribute To Robert Sund edited by Allen Frost
    and Paul Piper (2016)
and Light poetry by Paul Piper (2016)

Coming Soon

In the Valley of Mystic Light: An Oral History
  of the Skagit Valley Arts Scene edited by Claire
    Swedberg & Rita Hupy (2017)
Go with the Flow: A Tribute to Clyde Sanborn
  edited by Allen Frost (2017)

I hope you have enjoyed these books. There are
more on the way.

www.ingramcontent.com/pod-product-compliance
Lightning Source LLC
Chambersburg PA
CBHW030414120726
47904CB00007B/2275